Too good to be true?

He came close, not quite close enough to touch, but close enough for Audrey to see every detail of him. He was an amazing animal. His face was long, lean, and elegant, and his eyes were as blue as Audrey's. The ruff of long hair around his neck was white but with the same unreal silver sparkle as the rest of him.

"You are the most beautiful dog in the world," she whispered.

His plumed tail began to wave. He danced around her, but stayed just beyond her reach when she tried to touch him.

Shadows

by LYNN HALL

Illustrated by Dave Henderson

BULLSEYE BOOKS • ALFRED A. KNOPF

NEW YORK

1

***a**udrey slammed the cookbook* shut and hit it with her fist.

"I hate the people who write these books," she shouted. Her father wasn't home yet, so she could get away with shouting in the house. King wagged his tail and agreed with her. He was lying under the table, or in front of the stove. He was imaginary, so his position moved when Audrey moved.

"You'd think a cookbook would tell

you how to cook pork chops and potatoes, wouldn't you?" she asked him.
"But all it has is recipes. It doesn't tell
what you're supposed to do to cook
the potatoes in the first place. I don't
know if I'm supposed to peel them or
not, or put them in water, or how long
to cook them, or anything."

She felt like bawling, she was so
mad at the cookbook people, but her
eyes were all dried up from the last
few days.

She sat on the kitchen floor and put
her arms around King's imaginary
neck. She didn't feel anything but
empty air. A few years ago she would
have been able to feel him. Almost.

"This is the worst day of my life,"
she told King. "I know I said that
yesterday and the day before and the
day before. But yesterday everybody
at school was so nice to me. And the
day before that was the funeral, and
there was lots to do and lots to think
about. And before that were the two

days she was dead, but she didn't seem dead, King. I could still see her, and she was somewhere, even if she wasn't standing up and moving and talking. But today people acted as though everything was back to normal. And it isn't. And I can't feel you anymore when I need to hug you. I'm outgrowing you, aren't I?"

The back door opened, and her father was suddenly there, frowning down at her.

"Why are you sitting in the middle of the kitchen floor, Audrey?"

Before she could think of why, he stepped right through King, and the dog disappeared.

"I was going to cook supper," Audrey said in a small voice.

"Sitting on the floor? You go outside and play. I'll fix us something."

Audrey stood up and tried again. "I wanted to do it for you. You have to work hard all day." They were her mother's words coming out through her mouth, and they lumped up in her throat. "But the cookbook didn't tell how to make potatoes. If you'll tell me how, I'll do it."

"I said go outside and play," he snapped.

Before she could gather her hurts together, he turned and sat down at the table. "I'm sorry, honey. I didn't mean to sound so crabby."

She looked down at the floor. "Okay," she muttered to him, but to herself she said, "If you didn't mean to, then why did you?" It was like the times her mother said she was spanking Audrey because she loved her. That never made much sense, either.

"We're going to get somebody, a housekeeper, if I can afford it. Or Aunt Alice, maybe. Somebody to be here when you come home from school, and to fix supper for us. You shouldn't have to do that."

His voice sounded strained, as though he were trying to hold himself together. Audrey almost went over and hugged him, but she didn't quite know how.

Instead, she said, "I'm not very hungry for supper, anyway. Could I just make a peanut-butter sandwich and take it out with me?"

"That sounds like a good idea," he said with relief. "I'll just take a look at my paper, then." His voice trailed off after him, into the living room.

"He's forgotten about me already," Audrey told King in her silent voice. That was another nice thing about an imaginary dog. You didn't have to talk out loud to him.

She made her sandwich and reached for some cookies, but there weren't any. Shrugging, she held the door open for King, then followed him outside.

Carolyn and Linda were across the street in Linda's front yard. They had one end of a long jump rope tied to a porch post, and they were taking turns, one working the rope while the other practiced her ins and outs. Audrey wandered over, out of habit.

"Do you want to take the other end?" Carolyn called to Audrey.

Audrey shook her head. She didn't feel like jumping up and down over a rope. You had to be happy to jump rope, and right now she felt too heavy. Besides, one hand was still full of sandwich.

Linda bobbed out of the center of the rope whirl and came over. The past few days Linda and Carolyn had acted tight around Audrey, as if they didn't know how to look at her or what to say. But today it was better.

"Don't you feel like jumping?" Linda asked.

Audrey shook her head. "I think I'll go somewhere. Maybe out to the gravel pit. Do you want to come?"

They both shook their heads. "I thought you were told not to go out on the railroad tracks anymore," Linda said.

"My dad never told me that—just Mom." Audrey didn't like the sound of her words. She turned away. "I'm going, anyway. Bye."

It felt good to get away from them. She crossed all the familiar backyards till she came to the railroad tracks, then turned right and walked along them. King was with her now.

"I wonder if I'm going to turn into a brat," she said. "I know I'm not supposed to be out here. Just because it was Mother who said it and not Daddy, that doesn't mean the rule is off now. Do you think I'm going to turn into a brat, King?"

She sighed. Now there was that to depress her on top of everything else.

She walked along one rail like a tightrope walker for a while. Then she walked on the ties, stretching her legs to step on every other one. It was a good place to walk, up high on the railroad bed. The backyards on either side were getting wider and more like country now. One had some goats tied out on stakes, and another had an old black pony. Midnight, she called him. But she didn't stop to visit him today.

After the last of the backyards she followed the narrow path that led through the head-high weeds to the gravel pit. It was a mountain range in Audrey's eyes, with a ring of gravel-pile mountains circling a beautiful lake. On this side of the lake the gravel piles had been there so long they were growing patches of weeds and grass and even a few baby trees.

Audrey scrambled up the first mountain and sat down to rest her legs. Walking on every other tie always made her legs ache, but walking on every tie was worse, and walking on the cinders between the ties was worst of all.

From up here she could see quite a distance. Straight ahead, which was east, the farthest thing she could make out was the line of bluffs on the Iowa side of the river. The bluffs were pink because the setting sun was shining on them. When she looked left, she could see the gray and black shapes of Omaha and the city smoke against the sky. To the right were fields and lines of trees beginning to show fall reds and golds.

She turned around on her bottom. Before her was the sun, going down, and a shape in front of the sun. It was an animal, standing on the peak of the mountain across the lake. It looked like a dog, but her eyes were watering from looking into the sun, and she couldn't be sure.

She stood and put her hands up to shade her eyes. Just then the animal moved a bit, and suddenly she could see him clearly, shining silvery in the sun. He was a collie, but unlike any she had ever seen. His coat was silver blue, flecked with black, and the fingers of the wind combed it into a froth.

He was looking straight at her.

She wanted to call him, but her voice wouldn't work.

The dog turned and began working his way down the steep side of his mountain, coming toward her. He moved so quickly, so smoothly, he barely disturbed the gravel or the weeds in his way.

"Hello," she said in a soft voice.

He came close, not quite close enough to touch, but close enough for Audrey to see every detail of him. He was an amazing animal. His face was long, lean, and elegant, and his eyes were as blue as Audrey's. One side of his face was black, and the other side was silver blue, like his body, with flecks of black and a touch or two of tan and white. The ruff of long hair around his neck was white but with the same unreal silver sparkle as the rest of him.

"You are the most beautiful dog in the world," she whispered.

His plumed tail began to wave. He

danced around her, but stayed just beyond her reach when she tried to touch him.

"Okay. If you don't want to be caught, I won't try to. Just don't go away, all right? Will you stay here with me?" She spoke invitingly and sat down on a grass patch.

The dog sat down, too, and looked at her with merry eyes. The tip of his tail moved against the ground.

"My name is Audrey Schultz. What's yours? Let's see. We'll have to think up one. How about . . ."

She thought of one name after another, but they weren't right. Finally she smiled and said, "How about Shadows? You look like shadows on the snow. Yes, I'll call you Shadows. I suppose you belong to somebody."

She studied him. He was neither thin nor dirty. His long coat gleamed, as though someone brushed it every day. Even his white feet were clean.

"You haven't been playing out here very long," she said wryly. "I never look that clean after I've been out here.

"Maybe whoever you belong to doesn't want you anymore, huh?" She knew that was unlikely. "Would you come home with me?"

She stood up. The dog stood, too, and swept the air with his tail. His bright blue eyes looked deeply and warmly into hers. For the first time in six days Audrey's stomach didn't feel tight.

"Please come and—" She was interrupted by the whistle and rumble of a train. The dog heard it, too. Suddenly his head sank, and there was fear in his eyes. He looked at her once again, with what seemed to be an apology. Then he turned and ran toward the setting sun, and Audrey couldn't see him or anything but the sun's glare.

She waited till the train had passed and gone; then she looked over and around every gravel pile that ringed the lake.

There was no sign of the dog.

*t*he next afternoon Audrey
stood on the highest gravel mountain
with Carolyn and Linda beside her.

"He should be around here somewhere," she said. "Here, Shadows.
Here, boy."

"I think you made him up," Carolyn said dryly. She never missed a
chance to tease Audrey about King.
Carolyn never had imaginary any-
things.

"No, I didn't," Audrey flared. "He

was here yesterday and he *was* a collie and he *was* black-and-blue spotted and he had blue eyes."

Linda said, "What're you going to do with him if we find him?"

"I don't know. Just prove to you that I didn't make him up. I'd like to find out who owns him if I could. Maybe nobody does."

"Maybe your dad would let you keep him," Linda said. "Now that your mother . . ."

Audrey looked away. She had thought of that herself. All last night, lying in bed, she had thought about asking her father if she could keep the dog if he didn't belong to anyone. She had a feeling he might say yes, but, much as she wanted Shadows, the thought of getting him that way made her sick. She kept remembering that terrible day, kept hearing her mother's voice saying, "Absolutely not. Town is no place for a dog, and don't you ask again." And then her own voice saying the unforgivable thing.

She kept seeing the picture of herself using her father's grief to get him to allow her the pet her mother had said no to. The picture of Audrey Schultz turning into a horrible person who would trick her dad like that.

No, she couldn't allow herself to have a dog.

"We'd better start back," Carolyn said finally. "If my mom finds out we came out here—"

Without warning, pain shot through Audrey. The rest of them had mothers. She didn't.

She forgot for the moment the other emotions of the past week: the shock of the death, the guilt at what she had said to her mother, the stark fear of facing the time ahead without her mother. All that was left in Audrey was the ache of the loss; gone forever were her mother's voice, the shape and feel and scent of her, the way she touched Audrey's hair and face with maternal authority. From deeper in her memory came the feeling of snuggling into her mother's lap, the softness of it, the utter peace it gave.

More than anything, she wanted to cry, but she was afraid of making Linda and Carolyn uncomfortable again and of losing their company.

She pulled in a long hard breath, then turned with the others and started back toward town, along the tracks. "I don't see what could hurt us out here," she said stoutly.

Carolyn said, "Bums. They're afraid we'll talk to bums."

They walked in silence for a way. Then Audrey said, "I think I'd like to talk to bums. They'd be interesting."

"What is a bum, anyway?" Linda asked.

"I'm not sure," Audrey said thoughtfully. "Old men who hang around railroad tracks, I guess." She turned for one last long look at the gravel piles, but they remained empty of life.

She heard Carolyn and Linda up ahead.

"What are you going to do tomorrow?"

"I don't know. What are you doing?"

Tomorrow would be a Friday, but it would be a gift of freedom because of a teachers' meeting. The two walking in front of her didn't bother to ask Audrey what she was going to do with her gift Friday. She already knew, and maybe they did, too.

That night Audrey went to bed early with her three new library books. She'd read *Billy and Blaze* so many times she knew the words by heart, but tonight she was in a mood for its pictures. And it felt so good to squirm down into the pillows and covers with the books. The world was no bigger than the circle of light from her bed lamp shining on the blankets over her knees.

From beyond that world came muffled conversation. Mother was in the living room with Daddy. No, that was all imagination. Audrey sighed.

Imagination.

"Did I just imagine Shadows, too?" she wondered out loud, forgetting to turn her pages. "He seemed real. But then, so did King—at least he used to, when I first made him up. But I always knew he was imaginary. Am I going crazy, do you suppose?"

She read all three of her books and finally fell asleep. Somewhere among her dreams a tall, distant figure looked down on her and said, "Girls who make their mothers die go crazy." The figure started to laugh a horrible laugh, and Audrey woke, sweating and trembling.

It was almost light out, so she got up and ate a breakfast of crackers and chocolate milk that was beginning to taste a little funny. On the kitchen chalkboard she left a note telling her father she'd gone for a walk and might be gone all morning. Aunt Alice was coming to take care of her for the day, but Aunt Alice was not a worrier. She would trust Audrey to be off on her own for a while.

The morning sparkled with a light frost. The sky was clear and brilliant, and the old, leftover moon was still floating around up there. Audrey felt better and better as she ran through the backyards and up onto the tracks. She trotted instead of walking, which made the spaces between every other tie come out just right for her legs. She waved to the goats and took a minute to stop and rub the old black pony's nose and feel his warm, wet breath on her hand.

It was such a good-feeling morning that Audrey was not at all surprised to see the collie lying atop a gravel mountain, waiting for her.

"I knew you'd be here," she called to him. "I knew I didn't make you up. And I'm sure glad I didn't. Come here, Shadows."

She reached for him, but he moved away, just inches, just beyond her fingertips. His tail waved his hello. He stretched his front half out along the ground, as though he were bowing to her. Then he leaped in the air and raced around her. The low beams of the morning sun shone through his coat and made a silver halo around him. The breeze ruffled his mane and the long feathering of hair on the backs of his legs. Audrey's hands itched for the feel of him.

But he danced away from her reaching arms.

"All right, Shadows. Come here and let's talk."

She sat down so he could know she wasn't going to grab at him. The dog bounded once more around her, then sat a little distance away. He stared directly into her eyes.

"I'll make you a promise. I won't try to catch you, if that's the way you want it. Okay? Just stay here with me. I don't have to go home for a long time today. We didn't have school because of a teachers' meeting. Where were you yesterday? I looked for you. I brought Carolyn and Linda because they thought I'd made you up. They're my best friends. Except for you. You're my best friend now."

The dog moved his tail. He opened his mouth to pant, but it looked like a smile to Audrey.

"Am I your best friend, too? Or do you have an owner that you love? Where do you live? I live at 141 West Windsor Avenue, Bellevue, Nebraska."

Shadows lay down. He lay like a majestic lion, head up, eyes fixed on Audrey's face. He seemed to be waiting to hear her talk some more.

"My mother died last Friday," she told him softly. "One week ago today. She died of something to do with her blood cells. I can't remember the word. It's a hard word to remember. She was in the hospital only three days. They wouldn't let me go visit her because I'm under twelve."

Shadows gave her a long, warm look.

"Do dogs have mothers? That's a silly question. What I meant was, do you remember anything about yours? Would you know her again if you saw her? Did you ever do anything terrible to your mother, Shadows?"

Suddenly she didn't want to sit still. She jumped to her feet and said, "Want to see me skip a stone?"

They went down the slope to the edge of the lake. It wasn't a real lake, just the water that collected in the huge holes where the gravel had been dug out of the ground. But it seemed like a lake. Audrey found some small, flat stones and shot them, one by one, out across the lake with that special snap of the wrist that made them skim on the top of the water, one, two, three times before they sank.

a good show dog. And he said I could have her if Mom and Dad said I could.

"So I asked Mom as soon as I got home, and she said town was no place to keep a dog. I tried to talk to her. I tried to tell her how much I *needed* a dog, but she didn't pay any attention. I told her Uncle Glenn and Aunt Alice live in town and they have seven dogs, but she just said that was different.

"I told her I'd pay for all the dog food out of my allowance, and she said I needed my allowance for other things. I said I'd do all the house-breaking, and she just kind of laughed and said how about when I was in school all day.

"Finally I started getting mad, Shadows. It seemed as though I was just screaming inside how much I needed that dog, and all she was thinking about was that it might be some bother to her, taking care of it. All of a sudden I felt that if she loved me, she'd know how important it was to me. I started yelling, 'You don't love me. I hate you. I wish you were dead.' I didn't really mean it, but I guess—I guess God must have heard me say it, because the next week—well, the next week she was dead." A shiver ran through Audrey. "Am I the worst person you ever knew, Shadows?"

She didn't dare look at him, for fear she would see in his eyes that he understood what she had told him, that he hated her, the way her father would if he knew. The way Uncle Glenn and Aunt Alice would.

She kept her eyes on the ground in front of her face, but she heard the dog stir. She felt him come close. A puff of his breath warmed her cheek.

𝓢aturday morning. Audrey stood in the living room in her pajamas and considered. The one thing, the only thing, she wanted to do was to get out of the house before her father woke, and go to Shadows.

But the pull of Saturday morning habit was stronger than she had realized. Saturday mornings were for changing the sheets on her bed, dusting and dust-mopping her bedroom, and taking all the small rugs out for a shaking. Mother would be dusting and vacuuming the other rooms and scouring in the bathroom. Sometimes they had raced to see who could get done first.

Audrey squeezed her fists tight. She wanted the old habits. She needed them.

Moving faster than she ever had before on a Saturday morning, she cleaned her room. Then she wrestled the vacuum cleaner around the living room and dining room. She smiled, remembering how it used to frighten her, that big, brown, roaring vacuum cleaner. She'd thought that if the edge of the rug got sucked up into it, the vacuum cleaner would explode. No more of that childishness now.

She was done by lunchtime, and the pleasure on her father's face made the morning effort worthwhile.

"Is there anything else I should do?" she asked him while she washed the lunch dishes. It had been an easy meal—soup—with not many dishes.

He smiled at her. "No, honey. You did a fine job this morning. You go on and have fun now."

She wiped her soapy hands on her jeans legs and ran.

Shadows lay waiting beside the gravel pit lake.

"Oh, good. You're here." She panted from the long run. She reached to touch him, but once again he kept to himself. Still, the happiness in his eyes was welcome enough for Audrey.

"I've been trying not to think about it," she told him, "but all morning I kept wondering if you were still going to be my friend. I know, in my head, that you're just a dog and you can't really understand what I told you yesterday. I know that. But still it's a relief to see you. I told you the worst thing there is about me, and you're still here."

He flattened his ears back into his silver ruff and gave her a huge, smiling yawn. His blue eyes looked deeply into her own blue eyes. He seemed to be trying to say something to her without words.

"You know what, Shadows? I think I'd better start trying to find out who you belong to. I love you so much already that it scares me. Maybe there's a chance your owner would let me have you or buy you. I'd do anything for that. I'd beg Daddy or Uncle Glenn or anyone who could help me. And if I knew where you lived, then at least if I couldn't have you myself, I'd always know where I could find you when I needed you."

She stood up. "Let's go home."

The dog stood, too. He wagged his tail and watched her face and waited for directions.

"Home, Shadows. Go home."

He cocked his head and watched her brightly.

"You're not going to lead me, are you? Okay, let's see. It must be one of these farms around here close. I can see one, two, three, four, from here. It's probably one of those. Come on."

At first the walking was easy. They crossed the same field as yesterday, skirting along the edge of the maple grove where their leaf house lay. This field was of cut hay so it was easy to walk. But the next one, lying between Audrey and the roofs of the farm buildings, was a cornfield. The stalks reached nearly twice as high as Audrey's head, and the rows were so close together that she had to push her way between them. Shadows refused to follow.

"All right, you wait here," she said, nodding.

After a long battle with the sharp-edged leaves of the giant cornstalks, Audrey came out into the open. She leaned against a fence post at the edge of the field and looked around her.

There was obviously no one at home. The garage stood open and empty, and a large, angry-looking dog was chained near the door.

As silently as she could, Audrey melted into the cornstalks and fought her way back to Shadows.

"They already have a dog," she told him. "So I'm sure that's not where you live."

They set off across country again, moving in a clockwise circle around the area of the gravel pit. The next farm they approached looked more inviting than the first. The house was large and neat, with two new cars parked behind it. It looked like the kind of house that might have a beautiful blue collie living there. Hoping and hoping not, Audrey said, "This could be it."

She turned to look at Shadows, but he was gone, except for a flash of blue color in the fencerow weeds.

"You wait here, then," she called. "I'll be right back."

For a long time she stood looking at the house. The truth was that she just plain hated going up to strange houses and knocking on their doors, especially to ask a silly-sounding question. She practiced the best words to use. She felt her heart thumping against her ribs. Finally she clenched herself up and marched across the yard.

A pleasant-looking woman answered the door. She looked like the kind of grandmother Audrey had always wanted. Audrey relaxed a bit.

"Yes?" the woman said.

"I'm sorry to bother you." Audrey's voice had a squeak in it. "But I was wondering if you happened to own a collie, a kind of gray and black—"

The woman frowned a little and shook her head.

"No, we haven't had a dog in years, not since the children grew up and left. Did you find a lost dog?"

"Yes, sort of. Do you know anyone around here who might have lost a grayish collie?"

The woman gazed out toward the barn roof. "Collie, collie, let me think. No, I'm afraid not."

Audrey was more relieved than disappointed. "Okay, thanks anyway." She turned and went down the steps.

"Oh, wait. Wait a minute. You said a sort of grayish collie? Let me think. It seems to me there was something a long time ago, something about a collie. Let me think."

Audrey stood and didn't breathe while the woman searched her memory.

Finally the woman smiled sadly and

gave up. "I'm sorry, dear. I just can't recall now. My memory isn't quite what it used to be. It was probably nothing."

Audrey said thank you again and left quickly. Shadows came to meet her from his waiting place in the fencerow, and they went on to the next farm in their clockwise circle. Again he faded back as she drew near the house. Again Audrey's questions earned no information.

Her legs weary, Audrey pushed on to the last house. No one there had ever heard of a grayish collie. With a feeling of having tried her best, she started back toward the gravel pit.

"You must belong to somebody around here, but I'm about halfway glad we didn't find out who. You feel more like mine this way."

As they approached the railroad tracks, Audrey paused. A train was coming, and she wanted to give it plenty of room. The noises of it hurt her ears, and she knew they frightened Shadows.

"We'll wait here till it's passed," she said. Shadows was staring with fear toward the sound of the onrushing train. The roar of it seemed to shake him to his bones. He lowered his head and vanished into the long grasses behind him.

After the train was out of sight, Audrey called and called, but no Shadows appeared. On legs trembly with tiredness, Audrey climbed the slope to the tracks. She turned toward home, then realized there were men's voices coming from the gravel pit. On a hunch she followed the sound.

Two men stood at the edge of the lake, fishing. She approached quietly and whispered, "Is it okay to talk?"

The older man said, "Sure, sis. We're not catching anything, anyhow."

"Do you fish out here very much?" she asked.

"Off and on. Have for years. Why?"

"I was just wondering—did you ever see a dog hanging around out here? A collie, kind of grayish with black spots?"

The other man laughed. "A gray collie with black spots? You been drinking, kid? Collies are brown and white. What's the matter—you don't ever watch 'Lassie'?"

His tone said he was teasing, so she didn't mind. "You never saw a dog like that around here, then?"

"Sorry, sis," the older man said.

"That's okay."

She went back and sat on the track to rest her legs for the walk home, and to think.

How come no one at any of those farms had ever seen Shadows?

How come the men who came to the gravel pit to fish never saw him?

How come Audrey Jean Schultz could find him just about any time she came out here, except when someone else was with her?

Was Audrey Jean Schultz going crazy after all, seeing dogs no one else could see?

"I know he's real, though." She picked up a cinder and threw it aimlessly at a tie.

"I'm not going crazy—but I am sitting out here on a railroad track talking to myself, aren't I?"

A grin broke through her worry. She got up and started home.

After supper that night Audrey settled into the big chair in the living room, with her notebook and colored pencils. Her father lay on the sofa watching television with his eyes closed, as he often did after supper. Always before, when Audrey was in a drawing mood, she'd shut herself in her room so no one would see her pictures unless she wanted to show them. But tonight she felt like being in the same room with someone, even someone with his eyes closed.

She drew a horse, trotting, with his mane blowing out behind him. It was pretty good. There were better horses already taped on her closet door, but this one wasn't bad.

Then she sat for a long time, her face pointed toward the television set but her mind not seeing it. She wanted to draw Shadows, not horses. But he would be hard.

"If you're imaginary," she said silently, "I wish you'd come now so I could see how your ears go."

It occurred to her then that she hadn't thought up King lately. Not since Shadows. She tried thinking him into the room. Nothing happened. She shrugged.

Shadows lying beside the lake with his head up, waiting for her to come— that would be the way to draw him. She began.

He was harder to draw than anything she had ever tried. His ears, how did they go? His head kept coming out wrong. She frowned and hunched and erased and worked, and finally there was Shadows, lying on the paper and looking at her and smiling the way he did. He still wasn't quite right, but he was definitely Shadows. When she shaded in his black splotches, he was perfect. Nearly. She leaned back and smiled.

"What are you grinning at?" her father asked.

She looked up, startled. "I thought you were asleep."

He sat up, and his hair stuck out from the pillow in spikes. "Just resting. Can I see your picture?"

Audrey took it to him, but she held her breath. She usually hated showing her pictures to people. Her mother had always said they were fine, which didn't mean anything because she said it whether they were fine or not. The art teacher at school usually praised them, but it was always scary to think she wouldn't, and Audrey felt strongly about her pictures. She wanted them to be perfect. She wanted people to say they didn't see how she could draw that well, and usually people just said, "You've got the legs too long," or something like that.

Her father studied the picture for a long time.

Finally Audrey said, "It's a collie. Lying by a lake."

"That's a very good collie," he said, and Audrey flushed with pleasure. "Are those spots on him, on his head there?"

"Yes. He has little black spots all over, and half of his face is black, and he has a little tan there on his cheeks and his legs, and white all around his neck."

Her father looked up and smiled at her. "That is quite an imaginative animal. I like the way you have his tail sort of swirling on the ground that way. That's a good picture. You should keep it."

Audrey grinned and glowed and went back to work. Maybe I can do an even better one, she thought. Maybe one of him standing on top of the mountain. . . .

*S*unday morning breakfast had always been waffles and bacon in the past, but Audrey was not ready to tackle waffle-making. Scrambled eggs turned out to be easier than she'd expected, though. Except for a few bits of eggshell that got in with them, the eggs made almost as good a Sunday breakfast as Mother's waffles.

"You cooked breakfast, so I'll wash the dishes," her father said afterward.

"Okay." She got up and started for the door. Shadows might be waiting.

"Don't go far," her father said.

She turned. "Why?"

"We have to be at Glenn and Alice's by eleven, and I want to stop and get groceries on the way, so we'll have to leave here in about an hour."

Audrey's face drooped. "Do I have to go?"

Her father looked at her closely for the first time all morning. "What do you mean, do you have to go? I thought you loved to go there."

"Well, I do. I just . . . "

He disappeared behind the Sunday paper. "Yes, you do have to go. I want to watch the football game on their color set, and their feelings would be hurt if you didn't come, too."

Audrey sighed and set Shadows back in her mind for Monday after school.

The drive through Omaha always took forever. Today it took even longer. There were groceries to stop for, and gas to stop for, and traffic in the way. Audrey sat, holding her drawing of Shadows and watching out the window as the blocks went by.

Uncle Glenn met them at the door. He was the biggest man Audrey knew, and he had a funny combination of young face and bald head and freckles on his lips.

"How's my best girl?" He gave Audrey a hard one-arm hug, and she smiled all over her face.

"Jack," Uncle Glenn said to her father. "How're you doing?" It was more than a casual greeting. Audrey looked back and forth at their faces and saw, for the first time, that the two brothers loved each other. It was hard to remember they were brothers, they were so old. But seeing the caring on Uncle Glenn's face gave Audrey a safe feeling.

Aunt Alice looked around the corner from the kitchen and called something pleasant to them. She was tall, too, and she had an old-looking face with young-looking hair, just the opposite of Uncle Glenn. Her hair was in a long ponytail down her back.

"Dinner won't be for a little while yet," Aunt Alice called.

Audrey caught Uncle Glenn's attention. "Can I go look at the puppies?"

He nodded but looked as though he wanted to talk to her father for a while, so she didn't wait for him to come with her.

The kennel was attached to the rear of the garage. It was a neatly paneled room with a little compartment for each dog. Audrey set her drawing notebook on the shelf beside the brushes and combs and went from dog to dog for pets and licks. She had just settled down in Cameo's compartment, with the four puppies scrambling over her legs, when Uncle Glenn came in.

"Ugly little rascals, aren't they?" he teased.

She just grinned up at him.

"Tell me how they're coming along," she said, scooching over to make room for him on the floor beside her. When Uncle Glenn explained details about his dogs, she didn't always understand, but she loved the sound of the words.

"Well, sir, let's see." He took a pup and stood him up, foursquare, and held up the tiny head and tail with his huge, freckled hands. "This is going to be the best of the males, I think. See that rear angulation? He'll have to be awfully good in the shoulder to compensate, but I think he'll develop. Then that little roan puppy . . ."

He chatted on, and Audrey tried to understand everything. When he was all talked out about his puppies, she reached behind him and got her notebook.

"I brought this to show you," she said. "It's a collie. I thought you might be able to tell me how to make it better." What she really wanted was for him to say it was perfect.

He took the picture and studied it. "That's very good. You're getting better all the time. I think the ears should be bigger, but you did a good job with the merling."

"The what?"

"The merling. The markings."

She looked blank. "You mean the little black spots?"

"That's called merling, and this's a blue merle collie. You see, the dog is genetically a tricolor, but with the merling factor, which acts as a—"

"You mean there really is this color of collie?" she interrupted. "I thought I just made it up."

He looked at her oddly. "How could you make up something like that? You must have seen one someplace, or a picture of one, maybe a long time ago, and you don't remember."

From far away in the house Aunt Alice called, "Dinner, you dog people."

Audrey rose but walked as slowly as she could back through the garage. She didn't want to give up Uncle Glenn's attention yet.

"Did you ever see a blue merle collie, Uncle Glenn?"

"Oh, sure. You see them at the dog shows fairly often. They're not a common color for pets, but I've seen some. There was one I remember, back a few years ago—ah, here you go, young lady." They were in the dining room. Uncle Glenn held her chair out for her and slid her up to the table as no one but Uncle Glenn could.

It was several minutes before Audrey could wedge a question into the conversation.

"Uncle Glenn, what were you going to say before about that blue merle collie?"

He looked blank for an instant.

"Oh, yes. Alice, remember that collie—oh, five or six years ago—that got out of the handler's kennel and ran away? That was a blue merle, wasn't it? Yes, I know it was, because it was one of the top-winning dogs in the country that year, and I remember it was the first time a blue collie had ever won the Omaha Specialty Show. Remember? The story about his running away was in the papers, and I went out one night and helped look for him with some of the kennel club members?"

Audrey laid down her fork and put her trembling hands together in her lap.

"What on earth is a blue merle collie?" her father asked, not really caring.

"Like the one I drew," Audrey said. "Spotted like that." She turned swiftly to Uncle Glenn. "Can they have blue eyes, ever?"

He frowned. "I think so. I'm not

just positive, but I believe they do have blue eyes sometimes."

"What happened?" she demanded.

"What? Oh, to the dog that ran away? What did happen, Alice? He got killed, didn't he?"

Aunt Alice nodded and passed the rolls. "I think he was hit by a car or something. Maybe we should talk about something more pleasant at the table."

Uncle Glenn pointed with his fork. "No, by golly, it wasn't a car. He got hit by a train. Out north of town somewhere. In fact, it was up around Bellevue where they found him, now that I think about it."

Aunt Alice glanced at Audrey's face, then said sternly, "All right, Glenn. That's enough of that subject. We are at the dinner table, after all."

Audrey picked up her fork, but only so she would look normal. Her mind was racing, digging frantically, trying to make sense of it. There had to be some connection between that dog and Shadows.

But that dog was dead.

Wasn't he?

*b*y the next morning there was still just one thing clear in Audrey's mind. She would have to find out more about the dog who died.

During lunch hour she climbed the stairs to the second floor, where the school library was. Ms. Barnett smiled at her as Audrey laid her books on the "Return" part of the counter.

"How's my best customer today?"

"Fine," Audrey said. "Do you have any books about collies?"

Ms. Barnett thought. "You might try the Terhune books. Albert Payson Terhune. They'd be on the lower shelf, about under the globe over there."

Audrey found the books, then came back thoughtfully to the checkout desk. "Ms. Barnett, if I wanted to find out about something that happened in Omaha several years ago, where would I look?"

"What kind of thing?"

"Like an accident."

"Would it have been in the newspapers?"

"Yes." Audrey began to hope.

"Then you could go to the main public library in downtown Omaha. They have all the local newspapers on file for several years back. You'd need to know about when it happened— the month and year, at any rate."

Audrey nodded and accepted her new stamped books. She did a good job of not looking so excited that Ms.

Barnett would ask what she was trying to find out.

All afternoon she tried to figure out a way to get to the downtown library after school. It was impossible. She had no money for bus fare and didn't know which bus to take or where to catch it or where to get off. And she would have to talk to Uncle Glenn again to find out more about when the accident happened. He was at work now and couldn't be called until after supper. All in all, it was hopeless for today.

But not for tomorrow, she promised herself.

As soon as she got home, she checked the money in her bank. There was plenty for bus fare. Most of it was left over from her last birthday money from her grandparents. She had been saving it for dog food in case she ever got one of Uncle Glenn's puppies.

Whew, she thought. I've got the bus

fare. Next problem, how to get there. Who could I ask about buses? Daddy, but he'd probably tell me I couldn't go. And if I told him why I had to, he'd think I was crazy.

She thought and thought, then finally went to the telephone book. Nothing was listed under "Buses." She didn't even know if the buses had any kind of office, but it seemed likely. Then she dialed Information.

"Could you tell me who I should call to find out about the buses?" she asked in a small voice.

"Local or long distance?" the operator snapped.

Audrey wasn't sure. "From Bellevue to the downtown library."

"That would be the Omaha Transit System. That number is 555-5817 if you'd care to make a note."

Audrey's heart had begun pounding against her ribs again. She dialed the number.

"Omaha Transit."

"Could you please tell me what bus I would take from Bellevue to the downtown library?"

"One moment please," the voice said. "That'd be the Seventeenth Avenue bus. It runs every twenty minutes. Get off at Fourteenth and Broadway."

"Thank you." She hung up with a feeling of victory. Nothing could stop her now. She looked at the kitchen clock—an hour till time for her father to get home. She grabbed her jacket and ran, across all the backyards and up onto the tracks.

Shadows was waiting on the gravel mountains.

After supper, when her father was safely involved in watching television through closed eyes, Audrey took the phone around the corner into the kitchen and called Uncle Glenn.

"Hi, sweetheart. What can I do for you?"

"Uncle Glenn, you know that blue merle collie you were telling us about yesterday, the one that got hit by the train? Do you remember when it happened, exactly?"

"Gee, no, I don't think so. What do you need to know for?"

"I want to look it up in the papers. It's important to me, Uncle Glenn. I need to know what month and year it happened."

"But why? What's it have to do with you?"

"Please, Uncle Glenn."

He was silent. Then he sighed. "Let me think. It was four, maybe five, years ago, I believe. Might have been longer. Might have been six—time goes by so fast these days."

"Do you remember the month?"

"Hmmm. As I recall, it was kind of cold weather, but not snow on the

She smiled and climbed the stairs.

At the first desk she came to, she explained that she needed to find something in an old newspaper. The librarian pointed her up some stairs. At the top of the stairs another librarian pointed her to a huge room at the back, and there a third librarian, a young man, finally got down to business with her.

"November of five or six years ago? Surely. Come with me." After some searching, the librarian laid two large, blue volumes, as big as newspapers, on a table.

"If you don't find what you're looking for in those, let me know," he said with a pleasant voice.

Audrey opened the first book. It was made up of newspapers, one for each day of November five years ago. She began turning the pages, scanning, looking for headlines that said "dog." There were none. She went through the second book. None there, either.

The librarian came back. "No luck? Can you tell me what you're looking for? Maybe I can help."

"It was a story about a dog that was lost and got killed by a train. It was a valuable show dog, a blue merle collie, and lots of people looked for it. My uncle said he thought it was in November five or six years ago."

The librarian chewed his lip for a moment, then said, "Let's try October of those two years and November of, say, four and seven years ago."

Side by side they leafed through more volumes. Audrey's eyes began to burn. Every now and then the librarian had to leave to help someone else, but he came back to Audrey's table and went on helping.

Eventually they covered October and November of five whole years. Nothing.

Audrey sat down and looked hopelessly at the librarian. "It's got to be in here somewhere, but I can't think where else to look."

"Are you sure about the month?"

Audrey thought. She tried to remember exactly what Uncle Glenn had said. "He told me it was cold weather but not snowy, and he said the dog was in town for the dog show, and that's in November."

"Is it always in November?"

"Yes, I think so." Audrey frowned. "Wait a minute. There's one in the spring, too, every year. I think it's around April or May. It's not as big as the fall show, but—"

"April or May?" the librarian said. "That might have been cold weather. It could have been a cold snap in April. It's worth a try, anyway."

The ache in Audrey's back and the burning in her eyes were forgotten. She took the first of the volumes the librarian brought, and again began scanning each page, not reading words but waiting for "dog" to hit her eyes.

And finally it did.

*i*t was just a small story at the bottom of a back page.

A four-day search ended today when the body of a valuable show dog was discovered south of Bellevue.

The dog, a purebred collie named Champion Blue Meadows' Banners Flying, was the target of a search that began Friday, after it was discovered that the animal was missing from the kennel of professional dog handler Frank Marinka, of Omaha. The dog had apparently escaped when a yard gate was left open. The search was led by Marinka and the dog's owners, Mr. and Mrs. Alexander Nickols, of Arvada, Colorado, and was aided by thirty to forty members of the Nebraska Collie Club and the Omaha Kennel Club.

The body was found near the Rock Island Railroad tracks, south of Bellevue. It is believed the dog was struck by a train and killed.

When asked the value of the animal, Mrs. Nickols said, "In money, probably three to five thousand dollars. To us, of course, he was priceless."

Audrey read and reread the story. It was clear enough. That dog was dead. Killed by a train. There could be no connection between him and Shadows. And yet, the coincidences were spooky. Her finding Shadows right where the other dog had been killed, and both of them being rare blue merle collies. She shook her head.

"Would you like paper and pencil?" the librarian asked.

Audrey shook herself to attention. "Yes, thank you."

She wrote down the names and addresses of the owners and the handler, and then, slowly, loving the sound of it, she wrote, "Champion Blue Meadows' Banners Flying."

Suddenly she realized it was dark outside the windows. The clock said nearly seven. She thanked the librarian again and got out of there fast. She ran all the way to the bus stop and, with her mind, pushed the bus all the way home.

What am I going to tell Daddy? she stewed. The truth, I guess. It can't make him any madder than anything I could make up.

But he was furious. She knew it as soon as she stepped into the house.

"Where on earth have you been? I was just about to call the police. You had me scared to death, girl. Don't you ever do that again, do you hear me? Where were you all this time?"

She tried to explain. But when she got to the part about going downtown alone on the bus, his face grew red with the coming explosion, and her voice ran down to a whisper.

"You get to your room. Now! March. And if you ever pull a stunt like this again, so help me . . ."

She ducked around him and ran for the shelter of her room.

For a long time Audrey was too full of rolling anger at her father to think about Shadows, but eventually things inside her calmed down enough for the dog to come back into her head.

Shadows.

Champion Blue Meadows' Banners Flying.

What was the connection between them? Anything? Nothing? All her imagination?

As she often did when she couldn't

sort things out, she got her notebook and made a list of the possibilities:

1. It is the same dog.

2. It's not the same dog. It's just a co-incidence.

She thought for a long time, hitting the front of her teeth with her pencil. There had to be more possibilities than that.

After nearly half an hour of staring at the two meager items on the list, another occurred to her.

3. Maybe I heard about the dog getting lost, and I mostly forgot about it, and then I imagined Shadows from sort of half remembering what I'd heard about Banners Flying.

That sounded like a good possibility. Her mind went on hunting. She thought about the dog getting out of the kennel, following the railroad tracks out of town, being hungry, and looking for food.

Suddenly there was another possibility.

4. What if Banners Flying had mated with another dog before he was killed? What if Shadows was a son of Banners Flying?

Carefully, trying not to decide too soon what she believed, Audrey went back over all four of the possibilities on her list.

If it was the same dog, how could that be? Maybe the body the searchers found was in such bad shape that they only thought it was Banners Flying, but it was really some other dog. That happens all the time on television. Mistaken identity. In that case, could he still be alive? The accident happened five years ago. He was probably only about three or four when it happened, since he was still going to dog shows. She knew from Uncle Glenn that older dogs get past their primes and retire. So Banners Flying would be only about nine or so now. That was possible.

She suddenly remembered something. Shadows was afraid of trains. He ran away from them. Could it have been that the body they found really was him, that he had been hit by the train but wasn't quite dead, only unconscious? That happens all the time on television, too. It didn't seem likely that Mr. and Mrs. Nickols would have gone off and left his body when they loved him so much, but it was possible.

Or—they could have taken him to the vet, and the vet said he was dead and put his body outside on the trash pile or wherever vets put dog bodies, and then the dog woke up and crawled away and got better, and the vet never told anyone. That sounded good.

Okay, now for possibility number two: It's not the same dog. That might be the easiest and most logical answer, she thought, but I just can't believe it.

So, possibility number three: I heard

about the accident when I was little. How old would I have been? Five. I didn't even know what a collie was when I was five, so how could I have imagined what a blue merle collie looked like? How could I have imagined all the details about him?

And besides, Shadows is real. I know he is. I'm not crazy. I made up King in my mind, but I always knew he was imaginary, and for a long time I kept changing my mind about what he looked like. He was even a lion for a while. But Shadows! I could *see* him. I couldn't have made up how his face is divided right down the middle with the black on one side. And I'd never heard of a dog with blue eyes. How could I have made that up?

Mother had blue eyes. Maybe she's changed—no, that's crazy. I can't think that. Shadows is a real dog. He has to be.

What's the next possibility? Oh, yes. That Banners Flying had a son. Yes, that might be it.

She rolled over on her back and thought about that one.

He could have mated with a dog around here. A farm dog of somebody's. Maybe when the puppies were born, there was this one with the funny markings, and the people didn't like him, so they threw him out or something, and a wild fox raised him. That happens all the time, too, in books.

But would he have been that friendly with me if he'd been raised wild? He never lets me touch him, and yet he's very friendly. He plays with me, and he looks at me as though he loves me. I don't think a wild dog would do that. And his coat is all brushed and beautiful, not full of dirt and burrs and weeds like a wild animal's.

But he could still be a son of Banners Flying. He wouldn't have to have been raised by a wild animal. He could have been somebody's pet all this time.

But nobody around here has ever seen him, except me.

He could live in town somewhere and just come out to the gravel pit to play, like me.

"Audrey?" Her father's voice broke up her thoughts. She slid her list under her pillow and said, "Come in."

He opened the door and brought in a plate of supper. "I thought you might be hungry," he said.

She looked at him warily, but took the plate.

"Does that mean you're not mad anymore, if I promise not to do it again?"

He sat on the edge of the bed, but looked past her toward the wall. "I shouldn't have yelled at you like that, and you shouldn't have gone off without asking me first. Do we agree on that?"

"Yes."

"And especially you shouldn't have been wandering around downtown alone, and especially not after dark. It's dangerous. You're a young girl, and it's just dangerous for you. Do you understand?"

She looked down. "I guess so."

"The thing is, Audrey—what I was thinking tonight when I couldn't find you was that if something happened to you, now, after your mother, if I lost you, too . . ." He shook his head and looked away from her.

Softly she reached over and patted his arm. "I won't do it again." She meant a lot more than that, but it was all she could say.

He got up briskly. "Fine, then. We won't need to talk about it anymore. Good night, honey."

"G'night, Daddy. Sleep tight. Don't let the bedbugs bite."

After he was gone, she sat cross-legged on the bed for a long time, smiling at the closed door. Then she ate. When the plate was empty, she fished out her list and went on.

It comes down to two main possibilities, she decided. Shadows is the son of that other dog, or else they're the same dog, and he wasn't killed after all. I have to find out. Or I have to *try* to find out, anyway.

She turned to a clean page in her notebook and began to write, remembering what she could from school about writing formal letters.

> *Miss Audrey J. Schultz*
> *141 W. Windsor Avenue*
> *Bellevue, Nebraska*
> *October 24th*

Mr. and Mrs. Alexander Nickols
Arvada, Colorado

She stopped to think. If Arvada, Colorado, was a very big town, the letter might not get there without a street address. But what could she do? She'd just have to hope it reached the Nickolses.

What are they like? she wondered. Are they young or old? Rich? Probably, if they have a five-thousand-dollar dog. Are they nice? Will they pay any attention to a kid's letter asking such dumb questions? I guess I won't know if I don't try.

Dear Mr. and Mrs. Nickols,

I am writing to you about your dog Champion Blue Meadows' Banners Flying. I hope you won't think I am crazy, but I think I may have seen your dog. I read in the paper that he was killed. Was he really killed, for sure?

The reason I am asking is that I recently saw a blue merle collie near the railroad tracks at Bellevue, which is where the paper said your dog was killed. I have seen him several times, and he is my best friend. He is very beautiful, and I love him, and he acts as though he loves me, except for not letting me touch him. I would think I made him up, because I used to have an imaginary dog when I was young, but I never had seen a blue merle collie before, so I don't think I made him up.

Another thing I was wondering, would it be possible that the dog I saw was a son of your dog? If so, I thought you might like to know about him, in case he would be valuable.

The dog I saw has black all on one side of his face, and the rest of him is grayish-blue with black speckles. He is white all around his neck and his front legs, and on his back feet and the tip of his tail. His eyes are blue. Did your dog have blue eyes?

I hope you will answer my letter because I'm a little worried that I might be going crazy and making up imaginary dogs and thinking they are real. My mother died two weeks ago, and she had blue eyes, too.

Thank you very much.

Yours truly,
Audrey Schultz

PS: Here is a picture I drew of my dog. I drew it from memory, so it isn't very good. Could you tell me if he looks like your dog? Thank you.

It would be at least a week, she told herself, before an answer could come back. If they got the letter. If they bothered to answer it. If they didn't just think she was some crazy kid and throw the letter away.

As often as she could that week, Audrey went to the gravel pit after school. Shadows was always there, waiting. They went for walks sometimes, to the leaf house under the maple trees, or just up and down the gravel-pile mountains around their lake.

They talked. That is, Audrey talked, and Shadows absorbed her words in his gentle, caring way, with his head cocked and his bright eyes fixed on her face.

"When I was in the Easter play at school last year," she told him, "Mother came to see it even though it was just for the other classes at school. She came tiptoeing in and asked Mrs. Markle if she could watch from the back, and it really made me proud. She didn't feel very good then, Shadows. She had to rest a lot. Maybe she was already sick, back then. Maybe she knew she was going to die, and that was why she wanted that chance to see me in the play. Do you suppose? I never thought about that before."

The dog seemed to radiate a glow of love. It warmed Audrey like a blanket of peace.

On Saturday they had a long, lovely afternoon together.

On Sunday it rained a cold, blowing rain, and Audrey had to stay home.

On Monday, when she got home from school, the letter was there.

*t*he envelope was marked "Air Mail." It was addressed to her, and in the corner was the tiny figure of a collie and the words "Blue Meadows Collies."

Audrey sat at the kitchen table with her coat still on, and ripped open the envelope. It was a long letter, typed in blue.

Dear Audrey,

Your letter just arrived, and I honestly don't know how to answer you. The drawing you sent does, indeed, look like our Banner. I cried when I saw it. Although it has been five years since his death, Banner is still sorely missed at our house. We have owned and bred many collies through the years, but none with the great heart and extraordinary intelligence that Banner had.

Unfortunately, there is no question about his death. We were in Omaha when he was found, and we brought his body home with us. He is buried here, with his father and grandfather, in our spruce grove.

I'm afraid there is no possibility, either, that the dog you saw is a son of Banner's. For several months before his death, Banner had a virus infection that made it impossible for him to sire puppies. The Omaha show was to have been his last time in the show ring before retiring to be our house pet.

Banner was unusually attached to our daughter Ann, who was in high school at the time he died. He had always been her dog, and the two of them were almost never apart. Ann was in the hospital with hepatitis when Banner was killed, and I have often wondered whether he had somehow sensed that she was ill, even though he was hundreds of miles away, and was trying to come to her when the accident happened.

I will tell you something I have never shared with anyone else, even my husband. While Ann was in the hospital, she had a dream one night, in which she saw Banner, quite clearly, in her hospital room. At the time she told me of the dream, none of us knew that Banner was not safely locked up in the handler's kennel. We assumed it was just a dream, but I find it a rather comforting thought that he might have somehow been able to come to her then, just for a moment, to say good-bye.

Audrey, I am probably too old to believe in such intangibles, but I have seen *too many things in this life that cannot be explained by any logical means. The older I get, the less certain I am that anything is impossible.*

I am enclosing a photograph of Banner, taken the day he won the National Collie Specialty Show. It is an extra copy, and I would like you to have it. I don't know what dog you saw, dear, but I would like to believe it was our Banner. I would like to believe that somehow he knew there was a girl who needed him, and that the great love he held for all people enabled him to cross over the invisible wall that separates us from those who have gone on to another form of life, which we call death.

God bless you.

Cordially,
Miriam Nickols

Audrey's eyes swam with tears. She blinked and sniffed them away, and finally she could see the photograph that had fallen into her lap when she opened the letter.

It showed a magnificent blue collie standing beside a sign that said, "Best in Show." Over his back was draped a blanket of roses, and beside him stood a silver trophy as tall as the dog. The girl behind him, holding his lead and smiling a teary smile, was undoubtedly Ann Nickols.

Audrey moved the picture closer and stared at the dog.

It was Shadows.

LYNN HALL, the award-winning author of more than 85 books for young readers, loves writing dog and horse stories above all others. She lives in Elkader, Iowa, where she breeds and shows championship Bedlington terriers.

Faith's got a problem with learning to ride—horses terrify her!

A Summer of Horses

by Carol Fenner

For 10-year-old animal lover Faith, the thought of spending an entire summer at Beth Holbein's horse farm is like a dream come true. But Faith has a rather rude awakening when she arrives on the farm and realizes that horses are much bigger, much more powerful, and much, much scarier than she had ever imagined. Just being near these gigantic beasts terrifies her! And, to make matters even worse, her boy-crazy older sister—who doesn't even like animals—proves to be a natural-born rider. It's going to be a long, hard summer if Faith doesn't learn to love horses—and quick!

"Likely to command a loyal following."

—*Publishers Weekly*

"A good coming-of-age novel."　　　　　　—*Kirkus*

A BULLSEYE BOOK PUBLISHED BY ALFRED A. KNOPF, INC.

He was as free as the wind...

Whinny of the Wild Horses

by Amy C. Laundrie

For young Whinny, life under the open sky is peaceful and easy. Home is Wyoming's Wild Horse Valley, and his father is the leader of the wild horses that call it home. All Whinny has to worry about are wolves, coyotes...and people.

But Whinny's idyllic life soon takes a turn for the worse. First he loses his filly, Starfire, to a rival stallion. Then he's captured by a mean rancher who's bent on turning him into Red Devil, a rodeo bronc. Will Whinny ever know freedom again—or is his life as a wild mustang lost forever?

"A satisfying, old-fashioned horse story...Laundrie tells her story with clarity, grace and authenticity."   —*Kirkus*

A BULLSEYE BOOK PUBLISHED BY ALFRED A. KNOPF, INC.